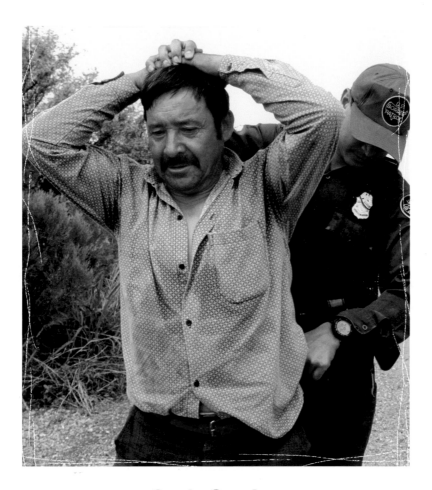

Taking Action TAKING ACTION AGAINST
Racism

Cath Senker

New York

Published in 2010 by The Rosen Publishing Group Inc.
29 East 21st Street, New York, NY 10010

First Edition

Editor: Camilla Lloyd
Consultant: Jayne Wright
Designer: Tim Mayer
Picture researcher: Kathy Lockley
Map: Ian Thompson

Library of Congress Cataloging-in-Publication Data

Senker, Cath.
  Taking action against racism / Cath Senker. — 1st ed.
      p. cm. — (Taking action)
  Includes index.
  ISBN 978-1-4358-5347-8 (library binding)
  ISBN 978-1-4358-5478-9 (paperback)
  ISBN 978-1-4358-5479-6 (6-pack)
  1. Racism. I. Title.
  HT1521.S384 2010
  305.8—dc22
                              2008053525

Picture Acknowledgments: The author and publisher would like to thank the following
for allowing their pictures to be reproduced in this publication: Cover
photograph:Zave Smith/Jupiter Images. Andrew Holbrooke/Corbis: 1, 13; Benjamin
Lowy/Corbis: 21; Bettman/Corbis: 9; CTK Czech News Agency/CTK/PA Photos: 14,
20BR, 25TR, 27TL, 30TR, 32TR, 36TL, 39TR, 42TR; David H. Wells/Corbis: 32; Ed
Kashi/Corbis: 16; Eric Gay/AP/PA Photos: 27; Haydn West/PA Archive/PA Photos: 22;
Howard Davies/Corbis: 36; Howard Davies/reportdigital.co.uk: 37; Hulton Archive/Getty
Images: 6; Images Source/Corbis: 4; Jacky Chapman/Photofusion: 31; Jed Leicester/
Corbis: 45; John Birdsall Social Issues Photo Library: 17; Judy Harrison/Photofusion:
33; Martial Trezzini/AP/PA Photos: 28; Martin Meissner/AP/PA Photos: 20; Nancy
Ney/Corbis: 40–41; Neville Elder/Corbis: 25; Nicholas Bailey/Rex Features: 35; Paul
Dymond/Alamy: 8; Peter Dench/Corbis: 10–11; Ralf-Finn Hestoft: 15; Reuters/Corbis: 5;
Richard Levine/Alamy: 29; Ruben Sprich/Reuters/Corbis: 26; Sam Diephuis/zefa
/Corbis: 38; Thierry Orban/Corbis Sygma: 12; Ullstein/Topfoto/Topfoto.co.uk: 30; Ulrike
Preuss/Photofusion: 18–

19; Will & Deni McIntyre/ Corbis: 42; Yoav Lemmer/POOL /epa/Corbis: 44; Yves
Logghe/AP/PA Photos: 23; Zave Smith/ Jupiter Images: 43.

Acknowledgments:
The author would like to thank the following for permission to reproduce material in
this book: p.5 Quote from *Preventing and Addressing Racism in Schools*, London
Borough of Ealing, U.K., 2003; p.7 Quote from *The Farmworker's Daughter* by Rose
Castillo Guilbault; p.11 In the Media from *The Australian*, October 27, 2006; p.13
"Terrorist Gangs" from Americans for Legal Immigration website; p.14 Mrs Zupková's
story by Laura Cashman; p.21 Facts from Unite Against Fascism, U.K.; p.24 Facts from
Human Rights and Equal Opportunity Commission, Australia; p.29
St. Petersburg Times, published February 27, 2001; p. 31 Quote from "Family:
Southside Schoolteacher Discriminates Against Muslim Girl" May 31, 2006 © 2007 by
News4Jax.com; p.32 From the Findings "Children's perspectives on believing and
belonging" published in 2005 by the Joseph Rowntree Foundation. Reproduced by
permission of the Joseph Rowntree Foundation; p.38 Mahmood's story from "Young
Voices—Mahmood," UNHCR, Australia; p.41 Action points from "We are experts—what
young people want," Teachernet, U.K.; p.43 Action points from ChildLine, U.K..

Manufactured in China

CONTENTS

Chapter 1

What is racism?

People in society are all different. Some of us are tall and some are short, and our skin and hair color vary. We have different ideas and we enjoy doing different things. Some people make judgements about people just because of how they look or behave, without even getting to know them. This is called prejudice.

For example, schoolchildren may look at another child in a wheelchair and think he is not very clever or good at his schoolwork because he is disabled. However, he might be a mathematics genius; it just happens that he cannot walk very well.

It is common for African-American and ethnic minority children to experience racism at school.

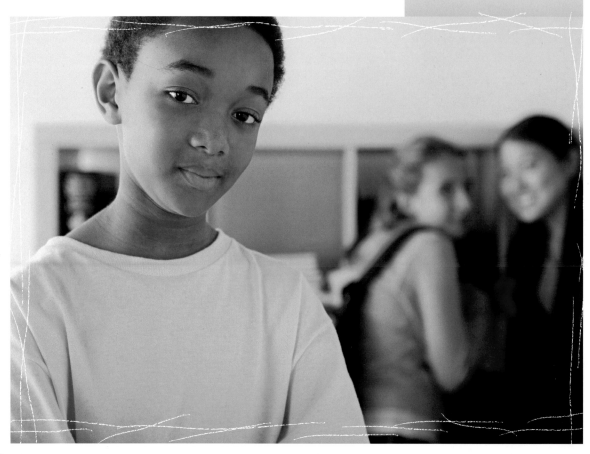

Some people are prejudiced against others who have a different skin color or are from a different ethnic group or culture. They feel superior to them. This is racism. Racism exists in many forms. For instance, in a classroom where most of the children are white, they might bully the few black children. People who are racist and have power in society can act against a whole group. An example of this happened in South Africa until 1990. Up until then, a small number of white people ruled over a majority of black people. The government kept people of different races apart. White people were provided with much better homes, schools, and hospitals than black people.

These extreme right-wing Hindus in Bhopal, central India, are protesting against an attack by Muslims. In the early 2000s, there were serious outbreaks of racial tension between Hindus and Muslims in India.

Racism around the world

Racism exists in most societies. In the United States, for instance, there is racism among white people against Hispanics, African-Americans, and Asians. It is not just white people who can be racist. In India, extreme right-wing Hindus believe that Hindus are superior to Muslims (who make up about one-fifth of the population). They say that India should be for the Hindu majority and are racist toward Muslims. Racism is an international problem, and it has a long history.

It happened to me

"When I was in primary school, they used to call me names in the playground all the time, like 'nigger.' They used to upset me and sometimes I would get so mad, I would fight and then I would get in trouble. I was always the one who got in trouble. They didn't do nothing to the ones that was doing it."
Child growing up in London in the early 2000s.

Where does racism come from?

Throughout history, there have been different kinds of prejudice. Sometimes, people did not trust others from abroad or people who had a different lifestyle. For example, the Roma (or gypsies) are traveling people who move from place to place. They left India in about the tenth century CE and moved around Europe. The groups who were already settled in Europe generally distrusted the gypsies and thought they were criminals.

European empires

A new form of prejudice arose between the sixteenth and the nineteenth centuries, when European countries took over large parts of the Caribbean, the Americas, Asia, and Africa. They ruled them as their colonies. In the Caribbean and the Americas, huge numbers of the indigenous population were killed, or died from disease. The European colonists needed to find other workers for their farms. They seized millions of Africans and bought them as slaves.

As rulers of the colonies, the white Europeans came to believe that they were superior to the black Africans they had enslaved and the other nonwhite people they ruled over.
The idea of racism based on skin color developed. It grew strong as the European empires reached their height in the nineteenth century and continued to rule their colonies in the following century.

Mass migration

After World War II ended in 1945, most colonies became free of European rulers but had been left extremely poor. At the time, European countries needed to rebuild their economies.

Police in London search a young black man in Notting Hill, London, after riots in 1958. Young white gangs who were hostile to the African-Caribbean immigrants had attacked their community.

The world in 1900

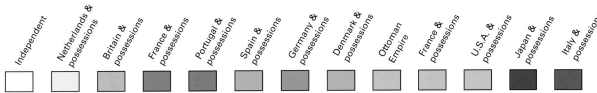

European countries invited the people of their former colonies in Africa, Asia, and the Caribbean to come to work in Europe. Although they were greatly needed, these new workers faced racism when they arrived. Many local people thought they were inferior and did not accept their different customs. In general, the newcomers were offered the dirtiest, most dangerous, and the lowest-paid jobs.

As in Europe, from the 1960s, the United States, Canada, and Australia changed their immigration policies to allow people from around the world to enter, rather than just Europeans as before. These countries provided good job opportunities for immigrants (people who migrated and settled). However, non-European immigrants often came up against racism in their new homeland.

In many Western countries (the countries of the Western world, especially Europe and North America), laws were introduced from the 1970s to make racism illegal, but prejudice is deep-seated and often rooted in people's upbringing, so racism is still with us today.

In 1900, large numbers of Western countries had a foreign empire. Britain had the largest empire, with colonies in many areas of the world.

Racism against migrants

Today, there is still racism, particularly against refugees and migrants. People become refugees when they flee their own land because of persecution, and attempt to seek safety in another land. People who move to another part of their own country, or to another land, are called migrants. Many international migrants (migrants from other countries) stay for a while to work and return home afterward. Some decide to remain in their new homeland. They then become known as immigrants. The prejudice against them is not just to do with skin color, although this is usually a factor. It is because they have a different culture, too, and are often seen as outsiders.

For example, some people in Western Europe have racist attitudes not only toward black, Asian, and Asian Indian immigrants, but also toward Eastern Europeans who have come to work—even though they are white.

This female Asian immigrant is a banana worker in Tully, Queensland, Australia.

It happened to me

"When I was five, Mom took me from Nogales in Mexico (by the border with the United States) to live on an isolated farm in California. Mom spent her life on the farm and never even learned English properly. My stepdad was poor and uneducated. He worked as a farm laborer for a low salary. If you were young and Mexican, it was understood you would work in the fields … My first time was when I was 11. But I wanted to go to college and have a good career. Eventually, I succeeded and became a journalist."

Rose Castillo Guilbault, growing up as a Mexican immigrant in the 1960s, found that Mexicans were expected to be farmworkers.

Many forms of racism

Racism can evolve in different circumstances. It is not always a matter of white prejudice against black people. Another example of racism comes from Israel, a country of many races. Since its formation in 1948, there has been conflict between Israelis and the Palestinians, who lost their country when Israel was formed. Many Israelis have racist attitudes toward Palestinians, believing they are violent and hostile and that it is not possible to live with them in peace. Likewise, many Arabs who sympathize with the Palestinians have racist views of Israelis, too. Racism can take many forms depending on where you are, the history of the country, and what is going on there.

Migrant Mexican workers pick strawberries in California in 1963. By 2004, one in every three workers in farming, fishing, and forestry in the United States was Mexican.

Chapter 2

Why are people racist?

No one is born racist, and racists can come from any type of background. There are many reasons why people develop prejudices. Some people might follow role models who are racist. Perhaps their parents or school friends are prejudiced. Some young people join gangs. If most of the members are racist, then a new member may feel the need to adopt the same attitude.

Ignorance can be a cause of racism, too. If people have never met individuals from other cultures and do not understand their customs, they may develop prejudices against them because they are different. They may hear fixed views, and believe them because they do not know any better.

Stereotypes

A stereotype is an idea of a particular type of person or thing. This idea is so widely used that, for many people, it has become fixed as "true," even though it may not necessarily be so. Stereotypes feature regularly in the media. For instance, some elements of the Western media can be accused of sometimes showing Muslims as people who follow a very strict and aggressive religion that supports terrorism, and who want to keep separate from wider society. Yet, the majority of Muslims are not like this. This is a negative stereotype, which is damaging and encourages racism.

People often make judgements about others without getting to know them. Many non-Muslims hold stereotyped views of Muslim women who cover up in public.

Blaming others

People may believe in stereotypes and hold racist attitudes but not act upon them. Others take action on the streets. They may join racist organizations, even if they are illegal. For example, in Russia since the 1990s, many skinhead groups have sprung up. They have neo-Nazi views, meaning that they follow Adolf Hitler's racist Nazi ideas that were developed in the 1930s. The skinheads believe in a "pure" Russian race and hate people from other countries and cultures.

Neo-Nazi skinheads are usually high school students, vocational students (learning a trade or skill), or young unemployed people. How do they become racist? Experts believe the skinhead groups have grown because of the economic crisis in Russia and the upheaval after the collapse of the U.S.S.R. in 1990. The young neo-Nazis blame immigrants for the difficulties in their society.

In the media

"You hear more and more stories of treatment of the Islamic community that really is substandard by members of our own wider community. It is vilification [describing them harshly and unfairly], picking them out of the crowd because they dress differently or they speak differently. If we are not careful, we risk raising a generation of Australians who will have a bias against Islam."

Australian Federal Police Commissioner Mick Keelty believes the media is responsible for fueling racist attitudes against Australian Muslims.

Scapegoating

Often, when a country is in crisis, people look for others to blame. This is called scapegoating—blaming a group of people for problems that they didn't cause. It is an important cause of racism.

Far-right organizations, such as the neo-Nazis in Russia, tend to scapegoat immigrants and claim that if they left the country, the difficulties would go away. In the U.S., too, far-right groups say that Mexican migrants are responsible for the increase in violent crime and even that they are terrorists. In fact, a 2005 study found that increased immigration led to a reduction in the crime rate. Immigrants were less likely to commit crime than Americans. They are simply being scapegoated.

At this demonstration in Paris, France, young Muslims protest for their right to wear Islamic dress, including the hijab (a headscarf worn by Muslim women and girls).

A border guard arrests a Mexican man who has entered the U.S.A. illegally. Mexicans are often scape-goated for problems in the U.S.A., but their work is vital to the economy.

Cultural differences

Rather than being openly racist against immigrants, some say it is impossible for people from different backgrounds to live together peacefully because of their cultural differences. For instance, France is a secular (nonreligious) country by law. Many French citizens feel that religious people coming into the country—mainly Muslims—are destroying the secular culture.

In 2004, the government brought in a law that forbade school students from wearing anything that showed their faith, such as the Jewish skullcap (a small round cap worn by some Jewish men and boys) or the Muslim hijab. This has led to racial tension, particularly between Muslims, for whom religion is a vital part of their life, and non-Muslims who fear changes in French culture.

In the media

"Our borders have become increasingly porous [easy to get through] from both the Canadian North and Mexico to the South. Illegal aliens [immigrants] are crossing them, virtually unstopped, in the millions every year. These crossings, which have become increasingly violent, are allowing multiple teams of terrorists to enter our country."

An organization that campaigns against illegal immigration in the United States puts out the message that illegal immigrants from Mexico are criminals.

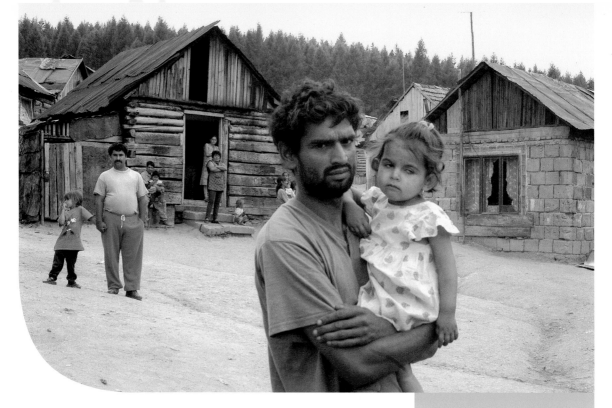

Roma and Travelers

The Roma and "Travelers" of Europe are affected by ideas about cultural differences, too. They have their own language, customs, and lifestyle. They move from place to place, unlike the majority of the population, who are settled. Many settled people hold racist views about them, believing they are lazy and likely to commit crime, or mislead people.

This Roma family lives in poor conditions in eastern Slovakia. As elsewhere in Eastern Europe, the Roma suffer from a higher rate of poverty, unemployment, crime, and disease than the majority population in Slovakia.

Rejected for being Roma

Somewhere between 150,000 and 300,000 Roma live in the Czech Republic, where racism against them is common. They are poorly educated and it is hard for them to find a job—around 70 percent are unemployed. A 2004 report described how the previous year, Mrs. Zupková applied for a job in the canteen at Hradec Králové University in Bohemia. She didn't get it. The manager told the employment office she refused Mrs. Zupková because she was Roma. She thought the Roma people were bad workers and was also worried that her customers would be unhappy if they saw a Roma serving food. In the first case of its kind in the country, the catering company was charged in court for racism.

TALK ABOUT

Look at these stereotypes about different races and kinds of people, and think of some others. Do you agree or disagree with them?

✳ African-American people are good at sports.

✳ Jewish people have successful businesses.

✳ Muslims are very religious.

✳ Women are better than men at taking care of babies and children.

For ideas on how to extend discussions, please see the Notes for Teachers on page 47.

Feeling superior

The catering manager in this case thinks that the majority of Czech people are better than the Roma people. Sometimes, people's pride in their country makes them feel superior to minority groups they see as outsiders, or to people from other lands. They claim they are trying to protect their way of life, which they believe is better than any other.

In the U.S.A., for example, 15 percent of the population are Hispanic, and more Hispanics arrive each year. Greg Letiecq, leader of an anti-immigration group in Virginia, complained that: "*It's the folks who come in and try to maintain the culture of the country they came from. They don't seem to embrace the American culture, the English language, the social norms of American culture.*" Such feelings can lead to racism against newcomers with a different lifestyle and culture.

This is a Hispanic neighborhood in Chicago. Hispanic people like to maintain their culture, but they like to mix with others, too. A 2006 survey showed that one-third of all Hispanic adults and half of Hispanic children spoke English very well.

Chapter 3

What do racists do?

As we have seen, racism can take many forms. It can affect people of all ages. At school, children might not want to work or play with others who have a different skin color or culture because they think they don't "fit in" with how everyone else acts and looks. Schoolchildren might behave in this way because they find it easier to stick with people who are like them. This is hurtful and unfair to those who are left out.

Sometimes children call other children names or tease them because of their background, what they look like, the way they talk, the clothes they wear, or the food they eat. This is very distressing for the children who are treated in this way. In extreme cases, a group of racist bullies might even beat up a child they've been bullying.

The effects of racism

In general, Muslim children in the U.S.A. have experienced a rise in racism since the terrorist attacks September 2001.

Racism can have a terrible effect on the individuals who experience it. It can make them feel sad, hurt, and extremely lonely. They may become depressed and lose their self-esteem. They might start wishing they were different, or think that somehow they are to blame or could have stopped the racist bullying from happening. Victims of racist bullying might even pretend to be sick so that they don't have to go to school. All these difficulties stop them from focusing on their schoolwork and from making friends. They may start doing badly and getting into trouble with the teachers.

Racist abuse can have a terrible effect on young people's lives, both inside and outside school.

Osama al-Najjar is a 15-year-old Arab from Jordan who lives in New York with his family. Osama shares his first name with Osama Bin Laden, the Islamist who ordered the attacks on New York on September 11, 2001. At school, Osama was constantly jeered at, and endured racist abuse because of his name. People called him "Bin Laden" and "terrorist." He says the teachers were worse than his classmates. His parents complained to the school but nothing was done. Osama began to do badly in his studies, got into fights, and ran away from home several times. Osama became so depressed that he tried to kill himself. "*I was just sick. I wasn't thinking straight. I had nothing else to take the pain away,*" he said. After he got better, he changed his name to Sammy in the hope that the abuse would stop. But he is still proud of his Arab background.

FACTS

✳ In the USA, black and white children have only been allowed to go to the same schools since 1954. But nowadays, growing numbers of African-American and Hispanic children in the poorest areas go to schools with only a few white students. In 2007, more than 1 in 6 African-American and 1 in 10 Hispanic children went to schools where more than 90 per cent of the students were non-white.

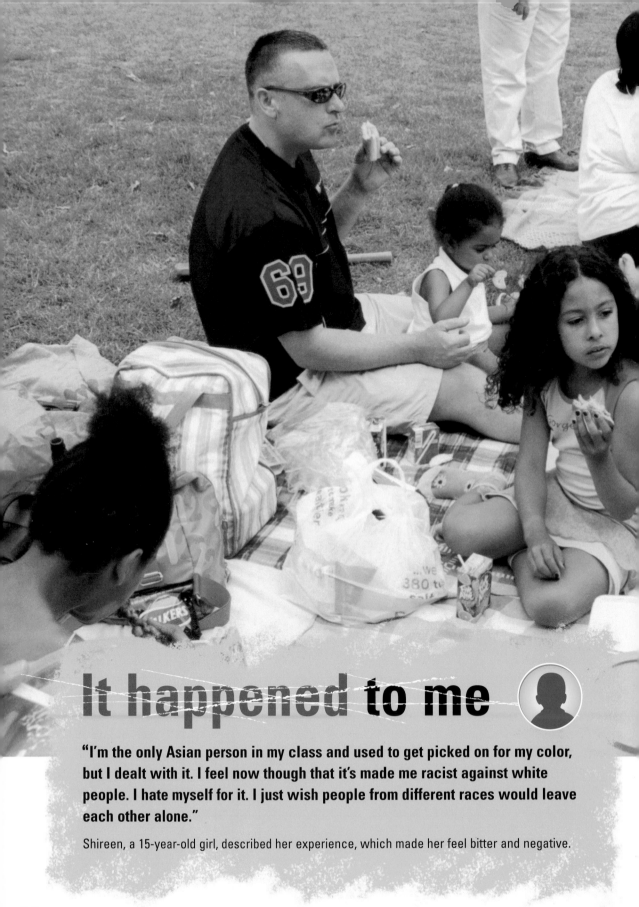

It happened to me

"I'm the only Asian person in my class and used to get picked on for my color, but I dealt with it. I feel now though that it's made me racist against white people. I hate myself for it. I just wish people from different races would leave each other alone."

Shireen, a 15-year-old girl, described her experience, which made her feel bitter and negative.

Mixed heritage families

Racism may not just be an issue at school, it can cause problems within the family, too. Children from mixed heritage families may have to put up with racism from one or even both sides of the family, because they are not like either side but a mixture of both. For example, some white people find it hard to accept an African-American person marrying into the family. On the other hand, there are African-Americans who are proud of their identity and do not welcome a white person joining the family. There is evidence that, over time, people tend to change their attitudes and become more tolerant.

White people suffer, too

Racism also affects white people. Mandy in the U.K. described her anger: *"I get really annoyed that lots of people at my school are racist toward Asian Indians. I'm not Indian, but have friends who are. My family doesn't like Indian people."* In the U.S.A., white kids who adopt black fashions and music tastes may be bullied for "acting black." It is clear that racism can affect lots of people.

A family group of mixed heritage. Britain has one of the fastest-growing mixed heritage populations in the world—despite the difficulties faced by couples from different backgrounds.

Organized racism

When racists get together, they can affect entire communities. Some people join groups to try to influence other people and carry out actions against people of a different skin color or culture. They may call them names, spray racist messages on walls, or smash the windows of their homes.

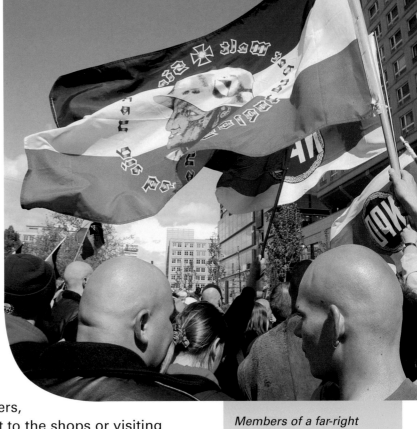

Organized racism can make whole communities feel frightened. If there are groups of racists hanging around on the street corners, the idea of even going out to the shops or visiting friends can become scary. People do not feel safe in their own home if the attackers know where they live. Sometimes, families feel they have no choice but to move away, hoping they will not be faced with racism in their new homes.

Members of a far-right organization in Germany on a demonstration. These neo-Nazis (modern Nazis) take their ideas from Adolf Hitler, who believed in a pure, white German race. This is why they sometimes attack nonwhite people.

Violence in Germany

Organized racism occurs around the world. It is an increasing problem in Eastern Germany, where neo-Nazi groups scapegoat immigrants for economic problems and blame them for the high levels of unemployment. They often target African people. In 2006, a group of neo-Nazi teenagers attacked a 12-year-old Ethiopian boy near the town of Magdeburg. They forced him at gunpoint to lick their boots. The attackers were charged in court. The judge said the only reason for the attack was the color of the boy's skin.

FACTS

* The far-right British National Party (BNP) became active in the Barking and Dagenham region of east London from 2001. Its campaign appeared to target members of the growing African communities whom it accused of taking away housing from the local people. The BNP campaign seems to have been the reason for increased racial attacks.

Source: Unite Against Facism, U.K.

Racist attacks, Barking and Dagenham, U.K.

2002–03	413
2003–04	486
2004–05	693
2005–06	699

Standing for election

Instead of using violence and attacking minority groups, some far-right organizations try to win political support for their views. They put forward candidates for elections and try to persuade people to vote for them. Usually, they are not open about their racism, because this may put people off. Instead they pose as respectable politicians who want to improve their community. They talk about the difficulties that affect ordinary people, such as poor housing and a lack of decent jobs. Instead of looking to the government to resolve these issues, they scapegoat immigrants and ethnic minorities. Some people, who want to find reasons for the hardships they suffer, may accept this simple argument, which leads to a growth in racism.

This graffiti on a wall in Warsaw, Poland, shows the Nazi swastika. Neo-Nazi groups are illegal in Poland, but they promote their views on the streets and on the Internet.

Race riots

An instance where far-right groups stirred up racism took place in Oldham, a town in northern England. Oldham has high levels of poverty and few job opportunities. Large numbers of Asian Indians live in Oldham, generally in separate areas from white people. Both Asian Indians and white people are affected by the economic problems.

In 2000, the far-right BNP became active in the town. The BNP said that the local government favored Asian Indians. The BNP encouraged white people to blame Indians for their misfortunes. Tensions rose until they boiled over into violent race riots in 2001. During the riots, up to 500 young Indians fought the police with gas bombs, bricks, and bottles.

A scene during the Oldham riots of 2001, in which cars were set on fire and windows smashed. The riots began when a group of racists attacked the Asian Indian community.

TALK ABOUT

Here are some different ways for teachers to deal with racist bullies at school. Which method do you think would work best, and why? Which methods would not work well?

✳ Ignoring the incident.

✳ Telling the children off and punishing them.

✳ Explaining why racism is wrong.

✳ Involving everyone in the school in dealing with the issue and trying to reduce racism through the curriculum.

Uniting against racism

After these terrible events, an organization called Oldham United Against Racism (OUAR) brought people together from local trade unions and voluntary, religious, and political groups. They decided to try to improve relations between whites and Asian Indians. The members went around Oldham handing out community newspapers, which explained it was untrue that Indians were being favored. They talked about the dangerous ideas of the BNP and produced materials to remind people about what happened in the Nazi Holocaust before and during World War II. OUAR held large public meetings to bring people together and break down the barriers between communities. The hard work of antiracist groups like this ensured that the BNP did badly in Oldham in the 2005 election.

These children in Belgium hold a banner saying, "Diversity is Reality". They believe that people should accept others who are different from them and learn to live with each other peacefully.

Chapter 4

Hidden racism

Often, individuals aren't deliberately racist, but certain ethnic minorities are still treated unfairly in society. Even though the law may say that everyone should be treated equally, people don't always stick to the rules. They might not mean to be racist, but certain ideas they have make them act that way. This is hidden, or institutional, racism.

At school

Hidden racism can exist in some schools. In the U.K., for example, the results of a report in 2007 showed that black pupils were praised less, told off more, and punished more harshly than others. Their teachers may not be deliberately racist; they might be acting in this way without thinking. There is a common stereotype that states that black children are no good at schoolwork. Black children might find themselves placed in the lower sets for lessons— especially the boys. In general, these groups have poorer resources, so it is harder for the children to do well.

FACTS

Research shows that there is hidden racism in some police forces. Even if individual police officers are not racist, they may accept stereotypes about ethnic communities. For example, in Australia, some believe that the police are more likely to suspect the indigenous Aboriginal population of committing a crime than the white population. The statistics below could show that the police believe the stereotypes, and so arrest and convict the indigenous population more readily.

✳ In 2005, in Western and Southern Australia, indigenous people were between 13 and 19 times more likely than nonindigenous people to be in prison.

✳ A 2003 study showed that in New South Wales in 2001, nearly one in five indigenous men appeared in court charged with committing a crime.

At work

Hidden racism also exists in the workplace. African-Americans and Hispanic people in the United States are often treated unfairly. They tend to live in poorer housing and go to worse schools than white people. When they grow up, they usually get lower-paid jobs. Even if they succeed in going to college, there are still barriers to finding a good job.

Most scientists in the U.S. are white or East Asian men. There are few African-American or Hispanic scientists. Erich Jarvis, a neurobiologist (a scientist who studies the nervous system) in North Carolina, was lucky to receive funding from an organization that helps students from ethnic minorities to go to college. His family was poor. *"We were lower middle class,"* he says. *"I was not like those students who got a car when they graduated. It was the other way around. I had to help my parents."*

In the United States, many African-American children live in poorer areas than white people and attend different schools.

Racism in colleges

Research has shown that, as well as the issue of money, there is a lack of role models for African-Americans and Hispanics to follow, so students from these groups are reluctant to apply to college. There is evidence that some university departments might not even take these students on, because they think they won't fit in. Those who do get a place may indeed feel like outsiders, and might not stay.

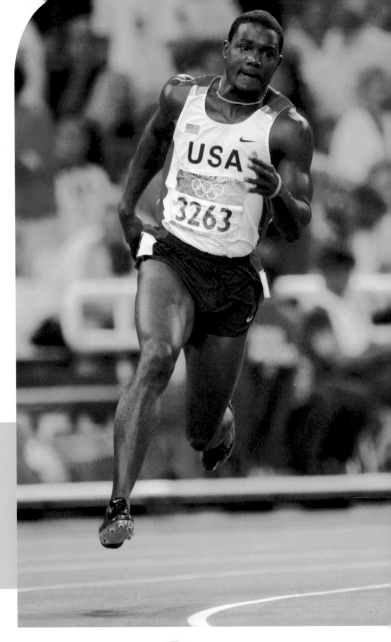

Justin Gatlin of the U.S.A. runs the 200-meter semifinals at the Olympic Games in Athens, Greece, in 2004. The stereotype that African-American people are good at sports may be rooted in the fact that poorer people have more opportunity to succeed in sports than in other professions.

TALK ABOUT

Although it is illegal to be openly racist in the media, this does not mean that all people are treated equally. Think about movies and TV programs, and compare the roles played by people of various races and cultures.

✳ Do you think that different people are provided with equal opportunities in the media?

✳ Do people of different races all have an equal chance to play powerful and interesting characters? Can you find any stereotypes?

Hurricane Katrina

Hidden racism goes on all the time in education and in the workplace. For many people, the disaster after Hurricane Katrina hit the New Orleans area in 2005 showed how big an issue hidden racism really is.

After the hurricane, the poorly maintained levees broke. (The levees were walls along the Mississippi River to protect New Orleans from flooding.) Around 80 percent of New Orleans was flooded. Thousands lost their homes. Most of these people were African-Americans who lived in cheap, low-lying housing. Large numbers were unable to escape New Orleans, because they were poor and did not own a car. There were hundreds of tragic deaths. One elderly man managed to drag his wife in her wheelchair to the roof of their home. When the floodwaters rose to the roof, he kept hold of her. Eventually, the flood pulled her away to her death. Help for people trapped in New Orleans was extremely slow to arrive. The rapper Kanye West said on TV that "*[ex-President George W.] Bush doesn't care about black people.*" Many Americans agreed that hidden racism within the U.S. government had been the reason for the slow response.

Amid the floods in New Orleans, anxious people wait on their balconies for rescue boats to come. A man directs the rescuer to the waiting families.

Chapter 5

What is religious prejudice?

Anti-Semitic vandals have drawn swastikas on this synagogue wall in Geneva, Switzerland. Half the people in a 2007 survey in six European countries thought that Jews were more loyal to Israel than their own country. This idea is a common stereotype.

Religious prejudice is based on difference, like racism. It usually affects people who look obviously different from the majority or have their own particular customs, such as Jews, Sikhs, and Muslims.

Anti-Semitism

One Jewish family was shocked to experience anti-Semitism (hatred of Jews) in the small town of Tampa Bay in Florida. They were called names, had filth put through their mailbox, and their car was damaged and painted with swastikas—the Nazi symbol. Their 14-year-old daughter was scared to go out to walk the dog. The family were determined to stay in their home, though. They explained their story at the town meeting and gained some support from their neighbors, and they put up security cameras to deter the vandals.

Anti-Semitism occurs in other Western countries, too. In the U.K., for example, there has been a rise in attacks on Jews. Sometimes people attack Jews because they link them to Israel, a Jewish country. A few people who were angry about Israel's war with Lebanon in 2006 went out and attacked Jews because of this anger toward Israel.

Children say their morning prayers at a Jewish school in the United States.

In the
media

After suffering racial slurs, smashed windows, and swastikas painted on their car over the course of a year, a Jewish family from the Tampa Bay area was deeply shaken. So they decided to attend a town meeting to tell their story and confront the neighborhood.

There, the MacNaughtons found support when they discovered that many of their neighbors were shocked at the news of this type of hate crime, which is uncommon in the 2000s. To try and stop the vandals, the local Jewish Defense League organized patrols and set a $1,000 reward for information about them.

The family also fought back by installing surveillance cameras and erecting a string of lights in the shape of a menorah, eight-feet wide. "It's a badge of honor," said Josette MacNaughton. "It's making a statement: I'm not afraid. I'm not hiding I'm Jewish. I never have, and I'm not starting now."

Source: *St. Petersburg Times*, published February 27, 2001

Islamophobia

Fear and hatred of Muslims, which has commonly become known as Islamophobia, is on the rise in Western countries. In the U.S.A., for instance, a 2006 poll found that 39 percent of Americans felt some prejudice against Muslims, and 22 percent wouldn't want Muslim neighbors. This prejudice has led to a rise in attacks on Muslims, including name-calling, setting mosques on fire, and
even murder.

Ideas about Islam

Why has this prejudice come about? It is partly because many people in Western countries think that Islam is a particularly strict religion. They believe that it is old-fashioned and has harsh laws against people who don't obey the rules. They think that Muslim women have no freedom. For example, many Muslim girls and women wear the hijab and dress modestly, covering their arms and legs. They dress in this way according to their religious and cultural customs. But some people in the West think that females are forced by men to adopt the hijab, and they

This mosque is in Berlin, Germany. Non-Muslims fear that Muslims are "taking over" by building their own mosques and businesses, although the proportion of Muslims in Western countries remains small.

These schoolgirls wear the Muslim hijab. There has been a big debate in many European countries over whether Muslim girls should be allowed to wear the hijab to school.

are not free because they cannot dress as they please. As well as the issue of women's freedom, some non-Muslims think that Islam is a violent religion that calls for terrorist action against non-Muslims. This belief has grown since the Muslim terrorist attacks on the United States on September 11, 2001. Al-Qaeda, the extreme Islamist organization that led the attacks, has threatened a war against Western countries. In response, the U.S.A. has led what it calls the "war on terror" to try to stop Islamic terrorism. Some people in the West are afraid of Muslims, because they think they might support Al-Qaeda. In fact, the vast majority of Muslims do not have extreme views and are completely peaceful.

It happened to me

Ten-year-old Alana Scott from Jacksonville, Florida, said she was not allowed to perform with her school orchestra because she wore a hijab. "We were on the school bus on the way to the concert hall. My cello teacher asked, *'Why do you wear that nun thing?'* When I explained, he made rude comments and said I couldn't perform because I wasn't wearing the right uniform. He said, *'Get off the bus or I'll have you and your mother arrested.'* I don't understand why he hates me so much. Sometimes teachers don't know everything. It made me feel horrible."

Religion in schools

As you can see, religious prejudice causes many tensions in society. In Western countries, these tensions have led to a big debate about religion in education. At school, you probably learn about Christianity, the main religion of your country. You also study other faiths and celebrate festivals from different cultures and countries. As one Christian child in the U.K. says, "*I definitely prefer a mixed school, because if it wasn't mixed, it would be boring. I wouldn't be learning about Islam or the Hindu or Sikh religions in Religious Education. It's fun.*"

Feeling alone

Yet some children feel anxious if there are only a few pupils of their religion at school. They would rather be at a school with others like them. A Sikh child says, "*I want to go to a Sikh school, because in this school there are so many Muslims. At Eid, most Muslim pupils stay at home and there are only five or six of us left in the class.*" For this reason, some parents prefer their children to attend religious schools, such as Catholic, Jewish, or Muslim schools. They want their children to be able to follow their faith freely at school and learn about their religion.

However, some people believe this stops children from different religions getting to

Sikh boys study at their temple. Sikhs often suffer racist abuse because they wear a turban. Some ignorant people think they look like Muslim terrorists, who also cover their heads.

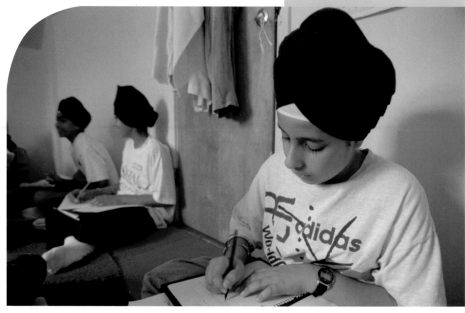

know one another and can lead to an increase in racism.

Learning about others

Whether or not children of different faiths study together, it is everyone's responsibility to get to know people of different religions. If you're from a main religion—or do not have a religion—you can try to meet children from different faiths. If you're from a minority religion, you can get more involved in the society around you so that people understand you better.

These children of different religions perform a Hindu Diwali play inside a Hindu temple.

TALK ABOUT

Think about the pros and cons of parochial or religious schools. Are these schools a good or a bad thing?

Pros

✳ **You learn about your own faith.**

✳ **You're protected from religious prejudice against your faith.**

✳ **You might grow up more confident.**

✳ **You can follow religious rules at school without being teased by others.**

Cons

✳ **You don't get to mix with others from different backgrounds.**

✳ **You may have to travel a long way to school.**

✳ **Children will not have a first-hand chance to learn about other religions.**

✳ **Many parochial schools are private, so only well-off families can afford to send their children to them.**

Chapter 6

Racism against migrants

People move to other countries for many reasons. They may move to find work, for a better life, or to feel safe. Today, a higher number of people live outside their country of birth than ever before in history. Yet migrants still make up only about 3 percent of the world's population—about 191 million people in 2005.

Migrant movements

The majority of migrants head for More Economically Developed Countries (MEDCs). One out of every four migrants lives in North America, and one in every three lives in Europe. Refugees form a small proportion of the total number of migrants—just 7 percent in 2005. Most refugees flee from Less Economically Developed Countries (LEDCs) to other nearby LEDCs.

As we saw in Chapter 1, migrants often encounter racism. It is not just to do with skin color, but also because of differences in culture, religion, and language. Migrants to Europe from Australia, South Africa, and the U.S.A. do not generally face the same level of racism if they are white and English-speaking.

This bar chart shows the 20 countries with the highest number of international migrants in 2005.
Source: United Nations Population Fund, 2006.

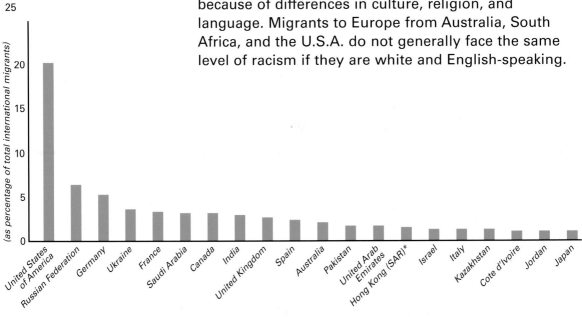

Special Administrative Region of China

Fears lead to racism

Racism can also arise because some people fear that the newcomers are taking jobs and homes from local people. Usually, migrant workers earn low salaries, doing the jobs that locals are not prepared to do. And although it may be true that there is a shortage of decent housing, the situation may be similar in areas without migrants. Local people often don't see the issues this way, though. They might also be scared that large numbers of migrants will change the culture of their country. Such fears are often whipped up by some newspapers and other elements in the media. This helps to explain why Eastern European migrants to western Europe may face racism even though they are white.

Poles in Scotland

This has been the case in some parts of Scotland. Between 2004 and 2007, around 40,000 Polish workers came to Scotland. They took on jobs as construction workers and farm workers, and also as bar staff and doormen in pubs and clubs. Some Scottish people resent the newcomers. On the weekends, some Scottish drinkers hurl racist insults at the Polish workers and occasionally even attack them. In 2007, one Pole, Patryk Mnich, was beaten up in the street in Pilrig, Edinburgh, and was left fighting for his life. However, many Scots welcome the Poles, who are bringing new businesses, skills, food, and cultural activities to Scotland.

Poland joined the European Union in 2004, giving Polish workers the right to work in other European Union countries. Within two years, around 750,000 Poles had come to the U.K. to work. Some opened shops, like this one in London.

Asylum seekers and refugees

Many people in Western countries are scared that there are not only too many migrants, but too many refugees as well. Only one-fifth of the world's refugees manage to reach Europe or North America. Even though they have fled persecution to move to a safe country, they are not always welcomed.

Claiming asylum

In Western countries, some asylum seekers are held in detention centers, like the one shown here. The government decides if they will be given asylum. In Australia, all asylum seekers are placed in detention centers.

When they first arrive, refugees have to claim asylum— the right to protection in a new country. Known as asylum seekers, they cannot work until their claim is accepted. (If they are refused asylum, they are supposed to return home.) Asylum seekers receive homes, health care, and education, even though they are not from the country and do not pay income tax. Many local people feel it is unfair because asylum seekers are getting "something for nothing." These economic arguments fuel racist thought and sometimes racist behavior. Yet most refugees are young and fit, and often well-educated. They want to work and contribute to their new country.

Asylum seekers at school

Although their parents are unable to work, the children of asylum seekers can go to school. It is good for them to mix with other children, but there are difficulties, too. As well as recovering from the upheaval of fleeing their country, they may be suffering trauma from terrible experiences. As one Scottish teacher explained, "*We always have to remember what some of these children have been through; the children from one family had watched their mother being killed.*" Some children are sympathetic and help the new children, but others—both black and white—may pick on them because they are different and perhaps can't speak the language. Many refugee children encounter racist bullying. If this happens, it is important for the staff and pupils in schools to try to stop it right away.

The young refugee in the middle has come to the U.K. from Ethiopia. It was a challenge adapting to school life after living in a refugee camp in Kenya for many years.

DOs & DON'Ts

✳ **Do talk about what it means to be a refugee.**

✳ **Try to find out about the country the refugees come from.**

✳ **Do put up some signs in the refugees' language and pictures from their country.**

✳ **Learn some playground and indoor games that don't involve speaking.**

✳ **Try not to say their name wrong.**

✳ **Don't ignore refugees at your school. Instead, plan a buddy for each new pupil.**

Hard to settle

Most refugees hope to return home when their country is safe again. For some, this isn't possible. If they come from a country that has been at war for decades, such as Afghanistan, they may need to make a new life in their adopted country. This is not easy. Mahmood came with his family from Afghanistan to seek asylum in Australia when he was 11. They spent three years in a detention center on Naura, a tiny island in the Pacific, before arriving in Canberra, Australia. He says, *"When you are on the journey, you think that this is going to be the hardest thing about getting to Australia, and that everything is going to be easy afterward. But once you get here, you realize that this is just the start. Adapting to a new society is like running a hurdle race. No sooner have you jumped over one than you have to jump over another one."*

A piñata is a brightly colored paper container filled with candy and toys. It is a Mexican tradition to play a game to break the piñata while blindfolded and free the candy and toys. Children play this game at birthday parties.

Many migrants also hope to return home after working for a few years. Some become immigrants and stay in the country. Over time, migrants and refugees gradually settle and integrate (mix with and become accepted) in their new country. The new communities make their own contribution to society.

Positive changes, reducing racism

In the United States, for instance, there has been a huge Mexican influence. Americans regularly eat Tex-Mex food, which is a mixture of northern Mexican and Southwestern American food. Foods from Mexico, such as chocolate, peanuts, and coconuts, are common, and salsa (a spicy tomato sauce) is now more popular than ketchup on American tables. Americans have adopted Mexican traditions, such as hanging a piñata at birthday parties. Celebrities originally from Mexico include the actress Salma Hayek and world-champion wrestler, Oscar Gutierrez.

Gradually, over time, as immigrants adapt to the country and local people get to know them, the tensions and racism are reduced. It has to be a two-way process, requiring effort from people already in the country and newcomers alike.

TALK ABOUT

Find out where the families of all the children in your class come from. Even if they were born in the country, perhaps their parents, grandparents, or great-grandparents came from another land.

✳ **What have people from each of these countries brought to your country?**

✳ **Have you been able to experience different cultures, such as food, sports, games, or music, because of families from other countries coming to your home?**

Chapter 7

What can we do about racism?

Some people face racism directly. They get picked on at school or in the street. Others feel under attack as a group. Perhaps they read or hear things that are rude about them. Some see people acting in a racist way, even though it is not directed at them.

What if it happens to you?

At first, you may have to deal with it alone. If someone shouts hurtful things at you, try to act calmly. Take deep breaths. Avoid shouting back or starting a fight. Although it is hard not to get upset or angry, it's worthwhile trying to remain calm. If you do not respond, the bullies may simply become bored and leave you alone. Then it might be best just to walk or run away, or if you feel confident, you could tell the bullies to leave you alone.

Remember that racism comes from ignorance. Don't be tempted to stoop to the level of the bullies and insult them back. Try to keep out of their way and spend time with your friends doing things that you enjoy. Think positively about yourself. You can show the bullies that you are strong and won't be put down by racism.

There are many good websites that can offer sensible advice on coping with racism.

Finding help

Sometimes you may need to get help from others. Talk to your friends, relatives, or a teacher you can trust. There are websites and organizations that can offer advice (see page 47). It helps if you know your rights. Racism is against the law, and racists can be punished, even if they are children.

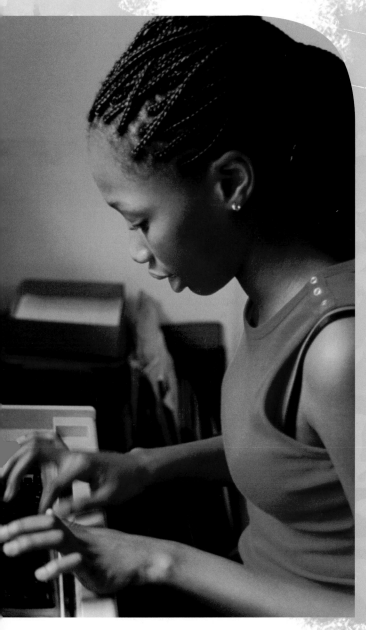

DOs & DON'Ts

Young people have explained how they would like teachers to respond to racism at school:

✳ **Do listen to how we feel.**

✳ **Do let us know that you are not racist and that you will help us.**

✳ **Do take action, however small the problem is.**

✳ **Don't ignore us because you haven't seen the racism yourself. It happens when staff aren't around.**

✳ **Don't jump to conclusions. Investigate the issue carefully before punishing someone.**

✳ **Don't assume that all the teachers understand about different races, cultures, and religions. All staff, including substitute teachers, should have training.**

Helping your friends

If you see racist bullying going on, don't ignore it. Remember that racism is not just to do with skin color. Teasing someone for wearing traditional clothes or not speaking your language properly is also racist. If your own classmates are saying hurtful things, you might feel able to talk to the bullies yourself. Otherwise, tell a member of staff you trust. Take action right away, or the bullying could get worse. If the situation becomes violent, it's best not to get involved in the fight. Get help immediately.

Once things have calmed down, offer your support to the person being bullied. He or she will want to have someone to talk to and to stick up for them. If you and your friends spend time with that person, he or she is less likely to be picked on.

A whole-school issue

The whole school community should tackle racism in school. The pupils who are responsible for racism must understand that what they are doing is wrong, and those affected should be supported. It's important for teachers to talk to the bullies. Some of them may be acting in a racist way to be part of a gang. They are scared that if they don't act like the others, they will be kicked out of the gang or lose face with the other members. Teachers need to understand their fears and encourage them to change their behavior; it is not enough just to punish them.

It is helpful if all children learn about the different countries their classmates come from, and their culture and customs. It can help to challenge racist ideas.

No one should ever stay silent about racism. It is up to all of us to tackle it.

DOs & DON'Ts

If your friend is suffering from racist bullying, read the action points below to see how you can help.

✱ Do listen to your friend talking about his or her experiences. It is important to be able to express anger and sadness about what is happening.

✱ Do take your friend's concerns seriously and show sympathy. Make it clear that you will help solve the problem.

✱ If your friend is scared to ask for help, find another person to tell a responsible adult about the bullying.

✱ Don't join in with the racists in the hope that they'll leave you alone if you do.

(Source: ChildLine, U.K.)

Every year on Holocaust Memorial Day, people around the world remember the Holocaust in which six million Jews died. As part of the ceremony in Jerusalem, Israel, Prime Minister Ehud Olmert lays a wreath.

Making a difference

There are plenty of positive things you can do to help stop racism. First, think before you speak. Be careful about how you talk about people from different cultures. In the United States, some non-Hispanics talk about everyone from South or Central America as "Mexicans," even though many are not from Mexico. This can be hurtful. Never laugh at a racist joke, just interrupt and say you don't find it funny.

Be open to learning about how different people lead their lives. Look for multicultural events such as carnivals and join in. Make the effort to get to know people from other cultures. You may be surprised to find how much you have in common, and you will learn a lot, too. Find out how people from different countries and cultures have benefited your country. You'll probably find that many of your favorite sportspeople, musicians, and movie stars come from different places.

TALK ABOUT

Imagine moving to another country with your family under difficult circumstances. Your language, culture, and religion are different from everyone else's. Think about some of the difficulties you would face. Which of these issues would you find the hardest to cope with?

✳ Learning a new language.

✳ Making new friends.

✳ Dealing with racist bullying.

✳ Not being able to practice your religion at school.

✳ Eating different foods.

✳ Missing your wider family and friends.

✳ Missing your home town.

Understanding the media

Don't believe everything you read or see. Learn to think carefully about what you see in the media. Try to work out if programs or articles in newspapers or magazines are being fair to different groups, or if they include stereotypes.

Antiracist activities

Antiracist organizations hold public events to oppose racism and promote understanding. For example, on Holocaust Memorial Day, people gather to remember the racism and anti-Semitism of the Nazis that led to the deaths of six million Jews. They talk about how to stop racism today. You might like to join a group that brings people from different backgrounds together, such as a sports team or theater group. You'll enjoy an exciting activity while doing your part to break down barriers between people and reduce racism in society.

At the Notting Hill Carnival in London, people from different backgrounds enjoy a colorful parade, lively music, dancing, and delicious food.

Glossary

African-American A term to describe Americans whose families originally came from Africa, usually as slaves.

Al-Qaeda An Islamic terrorist organization that wants American forces to leave the Middle East. Al-Qaeda also wants to set up Islamic governments across the Muslim world.

candidate In an election, a person who tries to get people to vote for him or her, so that he or she can join the local or national government.

colony A country that is ruled by another country.

detention center A place like a prison, where asylum seekers may be sent until the government decides if they are allowed to stay in the country as refugees.

ethnic group A group of people who share a culture, tradition, way of life, and sometimes language. An ethnic minority is a group of people who have a different culture, religion, skin color, or language from most other people in their society.

far-right organizations Groups that tend to be conservative in their outlook and to believe their country is better than others. They often have racist views toward people from ethnic minorities and migrants.

hidden racism When individuals are not deliberately racist, but the way things work in society means that people from ethnic minorities are treated unfairly.

Hispanic A person from a Latin-American country.

Holocaust The mass murder of Jewish people, Roma, and other groups by the Nazis.

immigrant A person who moves from their home to settle in another country.

indigenous people The people who belong to a particular place.

Less Economically Developed Countries (LEDCs) The poorer countries of the world, including the countries of Africa, Asia (except for Japan), Latin America, and the Caribbean.

More Economically Developed Countries (MEDCs) The richer countries of the world, including Europe and North America.

persecution Treating people badly, often because of their race, religion, culture, or beliefs.

poll Asking a number of different kinds of people their opinion on an issue in order to work out what the general view is.

race In daily life, the word *race* is used to describe a group of people who share certain features, such as black skin.

refugee A person who escapes to another country to seek safety from war, natural disaster, or bad treatment.

scapegoating Unfairly blaming a group of people for a problem in society.

slaves People owned by others and forced to work for them for no money.

terrorist A person who uses violent actions to achieve political aims.

trade union An organization of workers that helps protect their working conditions and pay.

welfare system The system in many countries that provides money, housing, and services to people who are very poor.

46

Further information and Web Sites

Notes for Teachers:

The Talk About panels are to be used to encourage debate and avoid the polarization of views. One way of doing this is to use "continuum lines." Think of a number of opinions or statements about the topics that can be considered by pupils. An imaginary line is constructed, which pupils can stand along to show what they feel in response to each statement (please see above). If they strongly agree or disagree with the viewpoint, they can stand by the signs; if the response is somewhere in between, they stand along the line in the relevant place. If the response is "neither agree, nor disagree" or they "don't know," then they stand at an equal distance from each sign, in the middle. Continuum lines can also be drawn on paper and pupils can mark a cross on the line to reflect their views.

Books to read

Choices And Decisions: Dealing With Racism
Pete Saunders and Steve Myers
(Stargazer Books, 2006)

Introducing Issues With Opposing Viewpoints: Racism
Laurie S Friedman
(Greenhaven Press, 2006)

Racism: The Impact On Our Lives
Cath Senker
(Raintree, 2003)

Web Sites

Due to the changing nature of Internet links, Rosen Publishing has developed an online list of Web sites related to the subject of this book. This site is regularly updated. Please use this link to access this list:
http://www.rosenlinks.com/act/raci

Index

Entries in **bold** are for pictures.